JUST CALL ME
JOE JOE

JEAN ALICIA ELSTER

ILLUSTRATED BY
NICOLE TADGELL

JUDSON PRESS ■ VALLEY FORGE

To my husband, Bill —JAE
For my Dad —NT

JUST CALL ME JOE JOE

© 2001 by Judson Press, Valley Forge, PA 19482-0851

Joe Joe's library book, *The History of the Negro Baseball Leagues*, is a fictional creation. The statistics and information attributed to it were gleaned from the following sources: Richard Bak, *Turkey Stearnes and the Detroit Stars: The Negro Leagues in Detroit, 1919–1933* (Detroit: Wayne State University Press, 1994). Wilmer Fields, *My Life in the Negro Leagues* (Westport, Conn.: Meckler Publishing, 1992). John B. Holway, *Josh and Satch: The Life and Times of Josh Gibson and Satchel Paige* (Westport, Conn.: Meckler Publishing, 1991). Patricia C. McKissack and Fredrick McKissack, Jr., *Black Diamond: The Story of the Negro Baseball Leagues* (New York: Scholastic, Inc., 1994). Jim Reisler, *Black Writers / Black Baseball: An Anthology of Articles from Black Sportswriters Who Covered the Negro Leagues* (Jefferson, N.C.: McFarland & Company, Inc., 1994). James A. Riley, *The Biographical Encyclopedia of the Negro Baseball Leagues* (New York: Carroll & Graf Publishers, Inc., 1994). Donn Rogosin, *Invisible Men: Life in Baseball's Negro Leagues* (New York: Atheneum, 1985).

The Bible quotation on page 3 is from the New American Standard Bible, © 1977 by The Lockman Foundation. Used by permission.

Vintage photography provided by the National Baseball Hall of Fame Library, Cooperstown, New York.

Elster, Jean Alicia.
    Just call me Joe Joe / Jean Alicia Elster.
        p. cm.
Summary: Reading a library book about the old Negro Baseball Leagues and the talented men who played in them gives Joe Joe the strength and self-esteem to do something difficult.
ISBN 0-8170-1398-9 (alk. paper)
[1. Self-esteem—Fiction. 2. Baseball—Fiction. 3. Negro leagues—Fiction. 4. African Americans—Fiction.] I. Title.
PZ7.E529 Ju 2001
[Fic]—dc21   2001029357

Printed in China.   07 06 05 04 03 02 01   10 9 8 7 6 5 4 3 2 1

"…and the sheep shall hear his voice,
and he calls his own sheep by name…"

—John 10:3

Joe Joe ran up the steps of the Bethune Branch Public Library. He pushed open the heavy wooden door with his shoulder. He was on his way home from school, but he had to make this one stop to see Mrs. Morgan.

Mrs. Morgan was a librarian. And, she was Joe Joe's very special friend. He came to see her every couple weeks. And when he did, she always had a book waiting for him.

Joe Joe skidded to a stop when he stepped into the main room of the library. He put his school books down on a table as he looked around for Mrs. Morgan. She was standing behind a desk with her back toward him. He crossed the room quickly.

Mrs. Morgan was taking books from a bin and putting them on a cart to be returned to the shelves. She seemed to expect Joe Joe even before she turned around to look at him.

"It's springtime," Mrs. Morgan said as she reached under the cart and grabbed a book. She turned and handed it to Joe Joe. "That means it's the start of baseball season. You like baseball, don't you?"

Joe Joe took the book. "Yes, ma'am," he nodded eagerly. "I even use the same bat my dad had when he was a boy."

"Then you'll like this book," Mrs. Morgan smiled.

Joe Joe held up the book and looked at the title: *The History of the Negro Baseball Leagues.* "Negro?" Joe Joe asked, tilting his head to one side.

"Today, we would say black or African American. The Negro Leagues were a group of teams for black baseball players. They formed in the early 1900s because it was the only way some very talented athletes could make a living playing the game they loved."

Joe Joe weighed the book in his hand and looked worried. "This is a pretty big book, Mrs. Morgan...."

She gave him a light pat on the shoulder. "Joe Joe, you've become a very good reader. Give it a try."

"OK. I'll try it. Thanks, Mrs. Morgan," Joe Joe said. He waved good-bye as he hurried over to the front desk to check out the book.

Then, he piled it on top of his schoolbooks and headed for home.

"Jo-o-oe Jo-o-oe!"

He glanced over his shoulder when he heard his name called. Kalia and Tyrone were running to catch up with him.

"Hey, Joe Joe, wait up!" Tyrone yelled.

Joe Joe stopped and put his school books down on the ground. His friends were out of breath when they reached him.

"Look what Mrs. Morgan gave me to read." Joe Joe handed the library book to Kalia.

"Negro Baseball Leagues?" Tyrone asked as he looked over Kalia's shoulder to see the pictures in the book.

"You know," Joe Joe answered, "the black baseball teams."

"Look at those old fashioned uniforms!" Kalia giggled.

"And look at that guy holding that beat-up wooden bat!" Tyrone smirked, grabbing the book from her.

"It's like my dad's bat from when he was a boy. He still lets me use it," Joe Joe beamed.

"I wouldn't play baseball with any beat-up bat. The guys today don't use an old bat like that either," Tyrone declared. He closed the book and handed it to Joe Joe.

"How do *you* know, Tyrone?" Joe Joe asked, shaking his head as he took the book back. "Anyway, why don't you guys come over and play some ball with me?" Joe Joe invited.

"Not with your dad's old wooden bat!" Tyrone yelled as he cut across a vacant field and ran toward his house.

"Maybe, after I finish my homework," Kalia shrugged. "See you later."

Joe Joe walked the rest of the way home alone.

By the time Joe Joe got home, he was hungry. He dashed into the house and dropped his books on the living room floor. Then he headed straight for the plate full of cookies on the kitchen table. He *loved* his grandma's sugar cookies.

"I *know* you aren't going to take a cookie before you wash your hands, Joe Joe."

It was his grandmother. She smiled as he quickly pulled his hand away.

"Oh … no, Grandma."

"Here, let me pop one in your mouth for you."

Joe Joe grinned and opened his mouth wide.

"Now, go wash!"

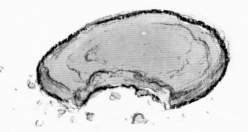

"Is Mama home?" Joe Joe asked as he headed for the bathroom.

"She left for the hospital just a few minutes ago. She's back on the evening shift for a while. But your dad's still here."

"All *right!*" Joe Joe exclaimed. "I'll go get the bat from the basement. Maybe Dad'll play baseball with me for a while."

As Joe Joe came up from the basement, he stopped short and then darted into the living room, dropping the bat as he shouted, "Brandon, be careful!" His two-year-old baby brother had the library book Mrs. Morgan had given to him. Brandon was holding it upside down and shaking the pages.

"That's a library book!" Joe Joe grabbed it out of his brother's hands. "It's a book about baseball," he explained, putting the book on a shelf, safely out of reach, and handing Brandon a picture book instead.

"Baseball?" Brandon repeated, tilting his head to one side.

"Yeah, baseball."

Brandon watched wide-eyed as Joe Joe picked up the bat.

"Bases are loaded. Joe Joe Rawlings at bat. There's the pitch! He takes a swing…"

"Joe Joe, now *you* be careful!"

Joe Joe dropped the bat at the sound of his father's booming voice.

"Let's take that outside," his father suggested, nodding his head toward the bat on the living room floor.

"Yes, sir," Joe Joe responded. He looked up quickly, his voice eager. "Will you play ball with me for a little while, Dad?"

"Sure, but just for a few minutes. I've got to leave for work. They need another welder at the factory on the afternoon shift. It looks like it'll be me for a while."

Joe Joe picked up the wooden bat. Then he got his library book from the shelf and handed it to his dad.

"Look what I got from the library. It's about the Negro Baseball Leagues. Dad, check out these pictures. Some of these bats look pretty worn out...."

"Joe Joe," his dad leaned down to look Joe Joe in the eye, "they had some mighty good players in those Negro Leagues. What they *didn't* have was a lot of money. Sometimes their bats got old and beat up. But they did just fine with what they had. And if *you'll* just wait for your pitch—*this* old wooden bat will do. It will do just fine. Now, let's go!"

They both grabbed a cookie from the kitchen and headed out the back door for the empty field behind their house.

Joe Joe came back into the kitchen after his father left for work. His grandmother was at the sink, cutting up a chicken.

"What's for dinner, Grandma?" Joe Joe asked, sniffing the air and resting the bat on his shoulder.

"Fried chicken, string beans, corn bread...."

Joe Joe grinned. It was his favorite meal.

"But, I need some paprika for the chicken. Go 'round the corner to Mr. Booth's store and get some for me." His grandmother put a five dollar bill in his hand. "You be sure to count your change."

He nodded and shoved the money in his pocket. "OK, Grandma." And he headed out the front door.

As Joe Joe headed around the corner toward the store, he heard yelling down the block. He looked up and saw some boys from the next block. Their blue sweatshirts and blue caps meant they were part of KC's gang.

The boys were running out of Mr. Booth's store. They were laughing and shouting and holding bags of chips, cookies, and fists full of candy. "Thank God they're running the other way" was the only thought that went through Joe Joe's mind. He didn't want to get into any trouble with them.

Joe Joe waited until KC's gang had turned the next corner before going into Mr. Booth's store. There were cans and bottles all over the floor. One of the counters was tipped over.

Without thinking, Joe Joe bent over to help pick up some of the cans.

"Get out of here! Haven't you boys done enough?"

Joe Joe looked up in shock. It was Mr. Booth yelling at *him*. His face was red, and his eyes were bulging with anger. He shouted at Joe Joe again.

"I said, get out!"

"But, Mr. Booth…" Joe Joe protested.

"Go on! I don't want any of you boys in my store—ever again!"

"But, I…"

"I said, *get out!*"

As Joe Joe backed away, still stunned, Mr. Booth sank onto the stool behind the counter. He held his face in his hands.

Joe Joe turned and ran home in tears.

He ran through the front door. He sobbed to his grandmother, "Grandma, I didn't do anything. Honest, I didn't do anything!"

"Joe Joe, what happened?"

Joe Joe told his grandmother what KC's gang had done to Mr. Booth's store. "And Mr. Booth thinks I'm part of the gang!"

"Oh, Joe Joe." Grandma hugged him tightly. "I'm so sorry.… I'm so sorry this happened."

She wiped a tear from his cheek. "Mr Booth has seen you in his store often enough. He should know that you wouldn't cause trouble like that.…"

Nodding and taking a deep breath, Joe Joe pulled away. "I'm sorry about the paprika, Grandma," he said quietly. Then he grabbed his library book from the living room and ran upstairs to his bedroom.

Lying across his bed, Joe Joe opened the book. Some words on the first page caught his attention.

There were already a few integrated baseball teams before the 1900s. In fact, the first African American to sign on with a major league team was not Jackie Robinson in 1945, as most people think, but a man named Moses Fleetwood Walker—"Fleet" Walker—in the 1880s.

"Fleet" Walker

Joe Joe sat up in surprise. "Hey, I didn't know that…."
His baby brother Brandon came into his room. He climbed onto the bed next to Joe Joe.
"Joe Joe crying," Brandon declared, pointing at his brother's face.
"No I'm not!" Joe Joe scrubbed at his cheeks. "Well, not now, anyway. Hey, listen to this, Brandon."
Joe Joe read aloud to his brother:

Fleet Walker made a name for himself while playing on his college team and later signed a contract with a major league club in Toledo, Ohio. But by 1887 the major leagues had decided not to hire any more black players and did not renew the contracts of the black players who were already on their teams.

"Boy, that's rough," he said, looking over to where his brother had been sitting. But Brandon had gotten off the bed and was playing with one of Joe Joe's trucks.
Joe Joe shrugged and kept on reading to himself.

Being "shut out" of the major leagues paved the way for the creation of the black teams of the Negro Baseball Leagues. In the early 1900s, leagues such as the Negro National League and the Eastern Colored League began to grow. Tens of thousands of fans showed up to see their favorite teams play against each other. They were happy to watch some of the best baseball being played anywhere.

Most teams rented ball park space for the regular season games. But a few team owners were able to actually build their own ball parks. It was an exciting time for African Americans in baseball!

Just then, Joe Joe heard his grandmother's voice call up the stairs. "Joe Joe, you and Brandon wash up and come on down for dinner."

"OK, Grandma!" Joe Joe called back, but he read a little more.

It was not an easy life. In order to make more money for their teams, owners sometimes scheduled two or three games in one day and in different cities! To do this, the teams usually traveled by bus. That was fine, except that many of the buses were not in good shape. They often broke down.

But the worst part for the players was traveling through the South because restaurants were segregated and would not serve African Americans. Hotels were segregated, too. Teams had to drive a long way to find a black-owned hotel or restaurant. Many times, team members ate and slept on the bus.

"It sure *wasn't* an easy life," Joe Joe thought to himself. "It wasn't right for them to be treated that way."

Joe Joe carefully marked his place in the book, closed it, and grabbed Brandon's hand to go wash up for dinner.

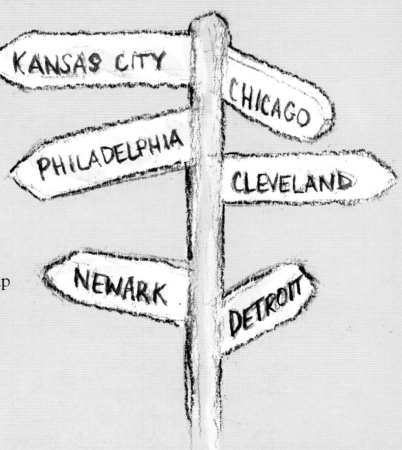

At the dinner table, his grandmother waited for Joe Joe and Brandon to sit down before she said the blessing. They bowed their heads.

"Thank you, dear Lord, for the food you have given us this evening. Thank you for keeping Joe Joe safe from KC's gang. Continue to watch over us. Amen."

"Amen," Joe Joe and Brandon echoed.

Joe Joe looked at his plate. The chicken looked different. When he took a bite, it did not taste quite the same, either. Then he remembered. It was missing the paprika. He didn't say much during the meal, thinking about what had happened at Mr. Booth's store.

Grandma noticed how quiet he was and asked curiously, "Is everything all right, Joe Joe?"

"Sure, Grandma," he answered.

But he did not enjoy his favorite meal that evening.

"Joe Joe. Come on down for breakfast!"

Joe Joe jumped out of bed. His mother was home and calling him for breakfast. He quickly washed and got dressed.

When he got to the kitchen, his mother was sitting next to Brandon and helping him eat his cereal. His father was reading the newspaper. They both looked up at Joe Joe as he sat down at the table.

"Joe Joe," his father said, putting down the paper, "your grandmother told us what happened at Mr. Booth's store yesterday. I could go over there and talk to him. But, I think *you* should be the one to do that."

"Aw, no, Dad…" Joe Joe shook his head quickly.

"You don't have to do it today or even tomorrow, but you're old enough now. You need to work this out between the two of you. Man to man."

"I don't think I can do it, Dad," Joe Joe insisted.

"You'll know when you're ready," his father answered. "In fact, before you go to sleep tonight, just *pray* that you'll know when you're ready."

Joe Joe didn't wait until bedtime. He squeezed his eyes shut and said a little prayer to himself *right then*.

"Dear God, I don't think I'll *ever* be ready, but if Dad is right, please let me know when *you* think I'm ready."

As Joe Joe opened his eyes, his mother stood and walked over to kiss him on the forehead. "Hurry up, now, honey," she said. "You don't want to be late for school."

Joe Joe made it to school on time, but that day, his classes seemed to last forever. He was glad when the last bell rang and school let out.

His feet were dragging as he walked home. It did not take long for Tyrone and Kalia to catch up with him.

"Hey, Joe Joe," Tyrone called out. "Wanna play some ball today?"

"No, not today."

Tyrone jabbed Kalia's arm with his elbow.

"I knew it! Didn't I tell you? He doesn't wanna play with that old wooden bat, either."

Kalia looked over at Joe Joe. "Really, Joe Joe?"

"No, that's not it. I just don't feel like it today," he answered in a low voice.

They looked at each other and shrugged. "OK. Then, see you tomorrow," Tyrone said as he and Kalia ran off.

"See you guys..."

When Joe Joe got home, his grandmother was on the telephone. He waved to her before running upstairs to his room. He got the book on the Negro Leagues and went out to the field behind the house and sat down under a tree. Brandon came outside dragging the baseball bat.

"Not today, Brandon," Joe Joe said to his brother.

Brandon tried to swing the bat himself, but it was too heavy for him. He put it down and ran back into the house.

Joe Joe shook his head, smiling a little as he opened his book and started reading.

Players like hitter Josh Gibson and pitcher Satchel Paige were heroes among fans of black baseball. But while Gibson could hit and Paige could throw, one player seemed to be able to do it all. His name was James "Cool Papa" Bell.

"'Cool Papa,'" Joe Joe thought to himself. "What a name..."

"Cool Papa" Bell began his career with the Negro Leagues as a pitcher. He threw knuckle balls, screwballs, and curve balls. He got the name "Cool Papa" from his teammates and manager who were amazed at how he stayed "cool" and calm during a high pressure game.

Then he hurt his arm and could not pitch anymore. That was when he became a star in the outfield and at bat. But he was best known for his speed. He was once timed circling the bases in only twelve seconds!

Bell also played more than twenty winter seasons in Cuba and Mexico. Players like Bell enjoyed playing on the Latin American teams where there was no segregation. There, Bell was treated as an equal among the other ball players. He and his family could live where they liked and eat where they liked.

But, "Cool Papa" always came back to play in the Negro Leagues....

Satchel Paige

Josh Gibson

James "Cool Papa" Bell

Joe Joe stopped reading right there. "Why would he come back to play in the Negro Leagues? Why didn't he just stay in Cuba or Mexico where they treated him right?"

Joe Joe heard his grandmother calling him in for dinner. Scrambling to his feet, he carried the book back into the house.

He was quiet all through that meal, too, but this time it was for a different reason. He was thinking about "Cool Papa" Bell.

"Why did he keep coming back?" Joe Joe asked himself over and over again. "Why?"

That night, as he lay in bed reading, Joe Joe got his answer.

"Cool Papa" Bell always came back to play in the Negro Leagues. He considered it an honor to be on a team in this country with some of the finest players in the game of baseball. No matter what problems he had to put up with in the United States—broken-down buses, restaurants that would not serve him, traveling to two or three towns in one day—he always came back. He never quit.

In 1974, long after he had retired from the game, "Cool Papa" Bell was elected to the Baseball Hall of Fame.

Joe Joe thought to himself, "Even when he wasn't treated right, 'Cool Papa' Bell knew that he and the other black players were the best athletes around. And he wanted to play with the best. *Nothing* could make him feel any different."

Then Joe Joe started thinking about himself. "No matter what Mr. Booth thinks of me, I know I'm not part of KC's gang. I didn't mess up his store and steal his food. I don't do stuff like that. I should be able to go in there anytime I want and buy whatever Grandma needs."

He remembered what his dad had told him. "*Go talk to Mr. Booth … Work it out … Man to man. You'll know when you're ready.*"

"I'm ready!" Joe Joe almost shouted out loud. His prayer had been answered. He smiled and fell asleep.

The next day at school could not go fast enough for Joe Joe. On the way home, Tyrone and Kalia had to run to catch up with him.

"Joe Joe, man, what's the rush? Wait up!" Tyrone panted after him.

"I gotta do something. Come by later on," Joe Joe answered as he ran off.

His grandmother was in the kitchen when Joe Joe got home.

"Grandma, do you still need that paprika?" he asked her.

"Why, I sure do …"

"May I go get it for you?"

She smiled wide. "Of course! Here's the money." She put a five dollar bill in his hand and squeezed it tightly. "Make sure you count your change."

Then she bent down and gave him a kiss on top of his head.

Joe Joe walked around the corner to Mr. Booth's store and took a deep breath before going in.

Inside the store, Mr. Booth was behind the counter with his hands on his waist, and he watched closely as Joe Joe walked by him.

Joe Joe went to the aisle where the spices were kept and reached for the paprika. He took it to the counter where Mr. Booth was standing.

"You know," Joe Joe began, handing Mr. Booth the five dollars, "I wasn't with those other kids who messed up your store the other day."

"I know ... I've seen you in here lots of times. I know you aren't one of the troublemakers. I'm sorry I yelled at you," Mr. Booth answered, holding out both hands apologetically.

Mr. Booth took the five dollars, put the paprika in a bag, and gave Joe Joe his change. "So, what's your name, young man?"

"Joe Joe Rawlings."

"Joe Joe, huh? Well, it took a real man to come in here like you did and stand up for yourself. You should call yourself Joseph."

Joe Joe thought for a moment. Then he answered, "One day, I think I will...."

He grabbed his bag and headed for the door. "But, for now," he grinned over his shoulder, "just call me Joe Joe!"

Mr. Booth smiled as he watched him leave.

Joe Joe ran back to his house and went straight to the kitchen.

"Here's your paprika, Grandma ... *and* your change."

"Thanks, Joe Joe." She hesitated and then asked, "How did things go with you and Mr. Booth?"

"Great! I talked to him 'man to man' like Dad said. I worked it out."

"I knew you could do it, Joe Joe!" she smiled in relief. She pulled him close for a big hug.

"Oh," she remembered as she released him, "Tyrone's out back waiting for you."

"Thanks, Grandma!" Joe Joe grabbed his bat and headed outside again.

Tyrone looked up as Joe Joe appeared, and smirked at the bat. "Joe Joe, you'll never be able to hit anything with that old beat-up wooden bat."

"You're wrong, Tyrone," Joe Joe answered with a big grin. "This old bat will do.... It will do just fine!"